ABBOTS HILL SCHOOL LIBRARY

R06374

to Carol with love

Text copyright © 1996 Roy Apps
Illustrations copyright © 1996 Amy Burch

The right of Roy Apps to be identified as the author of this work
and the right of Amy Burch to be identified as the illustrator of
this work has been asserted to them in accordance with the
Copyright, Designs and Patents Act 1988.

This edition first published in Great Britain in 1996
and reprinted in 1999
by Macdonald Young Books

Typeset in 15/22 Veljovic Book by Roger Kohn Designs
Printed and bound in Belgium by Proost N.V.

Macdonald Young Books Ltd
61 Western Road
Hove
East Sussex BN3 1JD

British Library Cataloguing in Publications Data available

ISBN 0 7500 2084 9
ISBN 0 7500 2085 7 (pb)

ELIZABETH FRY
AND THE
FORGER'S DAUGHTER

ROY APPS

ILLUSTRATED BY AMY BURCH

MACDONALD YOUNG BOOKS

1
Christmas 1816
A Den of Wild Beasts

It all started the day they nabbed Lottie. We were down at the market as usual. Ma and Lottie were doing a bit of soft – you know, passing forged notes, while I busied myself dipping my fingers into a few coat pockets.

I saw them first, great fat brutes with beady eyes.

"Runners!" I yelled.

Ma and me scarpered, but Lottie was slow off the mark – she was busy making eyes at a draper's boy.

And the runners nabbed her.

And that's why on Christmas Day of all days, Ma and me were hammering on the door of Newgate Jail.

"Liza," said Ma, "Christmas is a time for visiting your family and Lottie's about the closest thing you and me has got to family."

Newgate was quite a pretty picture from the outside. Until you realised there was something missing. There were no windows.

When you got inside you realised there were other things missing too, like beds, blankets and fires.

There was straw and there was filth
and a foul stench that hung in your
throat for ever. And there was a heap of
screaming, scratching, spitting women,
children and babies – all clawing at you for
money and stuff.

In the middle of the heap was Lottie.

"Gi'us a drink, Hannah Gunn! Gawn!" screamed Lottie. She didn't mean a drink of water neither.

Lottie was always the prettiest of Ma's friends, but now her face was scratched and pitted with sores.

Ma said, "I ain't got no gin!"

So Lottie grabbed her hair and tried to haul her through the bars.

We didn't stay a minute longer.

When we got outside, I was sick.

2

Winter 1817
A Great Day Out

I only ever saw Lottie once again. It was on a bright February day.

Most of London seemed to be out. The way everyone was all singing and laughing, you'd have thought we were off to the fair or something.

"Cor, don't take on so," I heard a mother tell her bawling kid, "this'll be a great day out!"

"Liza! Keep hold of my arm, girl,
before I faint!" Ma hissed at me. She didn't
want to be part of this 'great day out' any
more than I did.

They were going to see Lottie and so
were we. We were all going to see her
hanged.

"Don't you get no closer, Liza," whispered Ma. "I don't want to be seen, girl. If any of them runners clock me, mine'll be the next neck they'll be putting that noose round."

I shivered. The crowd became sort of hushed. Then the prison clock struck eight, the scaffold floor sprang open beneath Lottie's feet and a great ugly cheer went up.

I couldn't see properly. All the way home there were tears in my eyes. Tears of anger. I wanted someone to blame for Lottie being hanged.

We passed a running patterer selling his papers. "Last Pitiful Words of Hanged Forger Charlotte Newman!" he called, "as spoke to Missus Fry!"

"Who's Mrs Fry, Ma?" I asked.

Ma looked me full in the face. Her voice was bitter. "She's a do-gooding toff. She don't believe in hanging, does Mrs Meddling Fry. Oh no. Told Lottie she'd speak to the Queen herself to get her a pardon don't you know. And what came of all her fancy talk? Nothing. Lottie is dead."

I knew then whom to blame for Lottie being hanged. Mrs Meddling Fry.

I was so busy working out how to pay her back good and proper for what she'd done to Lottie if ever I got the chance, that I didn't take that much notice of the tall, stooping figure stepping back into the shadows at the end of our alley.

3
Summer 1817
A Warning

M a was scared. She was the one member of the gang the runners really wanted to nab. Ma was the clever one, you see: she could read. She even knew how to write letters.

The warning came all of a sudden: whispered to Ma by a barefoot street urchin with a scar across his cheek. "They're closing in. Get the next stage for Bromley. Friends will meet you."

"I knew it," cried Ma. "Lottie must've blabbed before they hung her! Reckon she must've told that toff Mrs Fry everything. She's a runner's nark, Liza, or else I'm a Dutchman."

Then she smiled, "Still, it's lovely down Bromley. It don't stink like London. There's fruit in the hedgerows and no runners to nick you!"

Down at 'The George' in Southwark, the stage was ready to go.

"Two seats inside!" Ma told the coachman, waving him a bank note – forged, of course.

"Here's to a new start!" Ma whispered. "You'll never get anywhere in life as the daughter of a forger."

There were two men in the coach.

"Where are you for, Ma'am?" asked one of them who was bent well forward, as if he had a stoop.

Too late, I remembered the stooping man who'd been lurking in the shadows the day we came home from Lottie's hanging.

"Ma!" She didn't hear me.

"We're for Bromley, Sir," Ma said in a superior way.

"Wrong," snarled the man, leaning over close to Ma's face. "First, you're for Newgate. Then..." he drew a long, twisted finger across Ma's neck, "you're for the drop, Hannah Gunn."

4
Summer 1817
Transportation Day

"Recently, I have been much exercised by representations made by Mrs Fry and the Society of Friends concerning public executions..."

Get on with it you dribbling old fool of a judge, I thought. Tell us Ma's for the drop, if you're going to!

"... You will not be hung. Instead you are to be banished with your child for a period of fifteen years to the convict colony in Van Diemen's Land."

Ma and me just stood there. Two months we'd been in the Compter – the local cells – waiting for a judge to send Ma to the gallows and me to Newgate.

"Now get them down to Deptford!" instructed the judge. "The convict ship *St Theresa* has just dropped anchor!"

"If I had my way, you'd have been hanged," sneered the turnkey to Ma as she clamped an iron fetter to her leg. "Very slowly. I blame that Mrs Fry. She's turning the judges soft. If she ever crosses my path I'll give her a piece of my mind, I can tell you!"

"Then you can give her a bit of mine, too," said Ma defiantly, "tell her from me, I'd rather I'd been hung than drowned at sea or starved to death in Van Diemen's land!"

The turnkey grabbed my leg.

"No!" screamed Ma, "you can't fetter my little girl! She ain't hardly eight years old!"

The truth was I was turned ten, though I suppose I looked about eight on account of being so small.

"She's a forger's brat how ever old she is!" growled the turnkey, slipping the heavy iron over my ankle.

Outside, we were dragged onto an open wagon for the ride down to Deptford Creek with the other local prisoners. I winced as the fetter thumped against my foot. Having such skinny legs, it was loose! Ma saw too and started to twist it to and fro. It cut sharply into my ankle. I wanted to yell out.

"I'm sorry, Liza. It's not much of a mother that brings her only girl to this."

"Ma..." I began. I was choking back the tears. I wanted to stay by her.

"Now go, girl! And do for yourself what you can."

All of a sudden, I felt the fetter slip off. "Oi! You turnkeys! You're all stinking pots of vomit!" yelled Ma.

While the turnkeys set about Ma, I slithered through their legs and was away before you could say Mrs Meddling Fry.

I should have got away from there sharp. But I couldn't. Every time I tried to run, a searing pain jolted my ankle.

I had to get one last look at Ma. I hobbled after the wagon from a safe distance.

It was soon joined by others from
Newgate and other London prisons, so I
let myself be swallowed up into the jeering,
taunting crowd of on-lookers as they
jostled the procession of convict wagons
all the way down to Deptford Creek.

There must've been a couple of
hundred or more convicts and their
children herded onto the tiny ship.

I caught a glimpse of one woman being
dragged up the gangplank by her hair. As
her face turned my way, I realised with a
sickening lump in my throat that it was
Ma. I thought she might've caught sight of
me, but I wasn't sure.

Then my eye was taken by a small knot of toffs, standing apart from the general rabble. Their leader seemed to be a stoutish lady in a plain dress and coal-scuttle bonnet.

The old man standing next to me gave me a nudge. "That's Missus Fry, that is," he said.

She was less haughty-looking than I'd expected. In my dreams, I'd seen her wearing silk and fine lace, with a disapproving sneer on her face, but as she watched the last of the convicts board the ship, she looked sad.

"Come on, pull yourself together, Liza Gunn," I muttered to myself. "Remember what that old nark did for Lottie and your Ma."

As the screaming and shrieking went on, I vowed again that I would get even with Mrs Meddling Fry, not just for Lottie's sake, but for Ma's sake too.

5
Autumn & Winter
1817
On the Run

B ut I didn't have much time to think
about getting even with Mrs Meddling
Fry. Ma's friends had scattered. I was on
my own. I had to get my food by stealing it
from market stalls and kitchens like any
other street urchin.

At night, we'd huddle up together for warmth under one of the bridges. I tried hard not to think about Ma, but every night she'd be there in my dreams.

All the other urchins worked in pairs or in gangs, but they wouldn't have me. My ankle was still playing up and I could be slow – dangerously slow – making a getaway. They didn't intend ending up in Newgate, any more than I did.

Still, it was autumn and though it was often wet, it was warm enough.

But when winter came, things changed.
The fresh fruit and vegetable stalls weren't
there any more to steal from. Cooks kept
their kitchen doors shut. A bitter wind
blew under the arches. I'd stopped noticing
that my feet were numb and that I
shivered all the time, even in my sleep.
I knew I was cold though.

One night I was wandering about
Haymarket when I came across a right
old brawl in the doorway of the Oyster Bar.

I slipped in under the flying sticks and
fists and found myself by the coat rack.

I felt around for the biggest and the thickest coat, pulled it from its hook and was out of the door before anyone had time to cry "thief!"

I put it on and straightaway its cosy warmth sent my body tingling. It smelt of cigars and perfume. I must've attracted attention, but I was too desperate to notice.

Until I felt the large hand grab my shoulder from behind.

"That's a fine garment for a young'un!"

I knew the sound of a runner's voice when I heard it. I ran.

I got as far as the corner of St Martin's Lane before a searing pain shot up my leg. My ankle gave way and I crashed to the ground.

I looked up to find myself staring into the ugly great face of a Bow Street Runner.

"On the streets are yer? Well I knows a nice little place for the likes of you. It's called Newgate!"

The vision of that filthy, seething, howling cess pit filled my head. I could hear myself screaming with terror. I must've struggled hard, for the next thing I remember was a thump on my head – then everything went black.

6

Spring 1818
Mrs Fry

I was having this dream about Mrs Meddling Fry. She was staring down at me and I was saying, "I'm going to get even with you!"

"You're... Liza Gunn, aren't you," said Mrs Fry.

"You ain't got nothin' on me, you runner's nark!" I heard myself saying.

"You have your mother's eyes – and her tongue," said Mrs Fry.

"Ma? What have you to do with Ma?"

"I visited her many times on the *St Theresa*. Two months they were berthed at Deptford. She gave me a letter to give to you, were you ever to turn up in Newgate, which she thought you might. I shall bring it to you tomorrow. Can you read? If not, you can learn in the Newgate School here as soon as you're a little better. Now Friend, you should try to rest."

I looked around. The Newgate of this dream was a very different place to the one I'd visited Lottie in.

The stench was still there, but nothing like as bad. It was less crowded and quiet! No one was swearing. I raised myself up and saw Mrs Fry talking to a group of prisoners and children. I tried to get up – but my ankle hurt.

Only then did I dare to believe that this Newgate wasn't a dream. This Newgate was real.

Next morning, Mrs Fry read me Ma's letter. It wasn't what you'd call long.

My Dear Girl, Liza, it said, *Mrs Fry is no more a runner's nark than I am. She has got us better conditions than we ever hoped for. I am sorry for all the trouble. Should I arrive safe and get settled, you may expect, care of Mrs Fry, another letter.*

From your loving Ma.

"Has she written?" I asked. I knew the answer, even before Mrs Fry shook her head sadly.

I started in Mrs Fry's Newgate School next day. I learnt to sew a little and to read of sorts, mainly from the Bible. This would be useful for me when I sailed, Mrs Fry said. For Van Diemen's Land was where I should've been these last months. I only hoped Ma had got there.

Every day I asked Mrs Fry if she'd had a letter. Each time she shook her head.

7

Summer 1818
A Future

My journey to Deptford Creek was not like Ma's. Mrs Fry had got chains and fetters banned and the wagons were covered, so we could tolerate the jeering passably.

Thanks to Mrs Fry, we all had a bag of 'useful things' such as tapes, pins and materials for making patchwork. We'd all have something to sell when we reached Van Diemen's Land.

We were given a comb – and of course, a Bible. I kept Ma's letter in my Bible and read it each night.

I was reading it the night we were due to set sail. Mrs Fry came aboard for a farewell visit. She strode over to me and thrust an envelope into my hand, a warm smile on her face.

"It arrived last night aboard the *Pegasus*!" she said.

My Dear Girl, Liza, I am well settled here. Thanks to Mrs Fry, I can sew and read better than I could before, so I can earn some money. I only have one hope, that some day I shall see you again.

Your loving Ma.

"You'll have no problem finding her in New South Wales," said Mrs Fry. "Walk cheerfully, Friend." Then she turned and hurried away.

"Mrs Fry!" I called. But she and the rest of the Friends were already leaving the ship. And my excited cries of thanks were drowned by the shouts of the crew as they raised the anchor from the river bed and hoisted the sails. I clutched Ma's letter tightly in my hand. I knew, that thanks to Mrs Fry, I'd soon be with her once again.